A Robot Instead

Tana Reiff

A Pacemaker® *WorkTales* Book

FEARON/JANUS
Belmont, California

Simon & Schuster Supplementary Education Group

WorkTales

Cover illustration: Terry Hoff
Interior illustration: James Balkovek

ISBN 0-8224-7156-6
Library of Congress Catalog Card Number: 91-70775
Printed in the United States of America
10 9 8 7 6 5 4 3 2

CONTENTS

CHAPTER 1

Sonny watched
as the next engine block
moved toward him.
It was his job
to drill bolt holes
into the new car engines.
All day,
day after day,
he drilled those holes.
Buzz, click.
Buzz, click.
Buzz, click.
Buzz, click.

Another engine block
headed toward him.
Buzz, click.
Buzz, click.
Buzz, click.
Buzz, click.

"Sometimes
I don't want to see
one more engine block,"
he shouted
to the next guy
down the line.
"Sometimes I get
real tired
of this same old job."

But working
on the line
at the machine shop
was Sonny's living.
This is how
he fed his family.
He had taken this job
to try something
besides welding.

Buzz, click.
Buzz, click.
Every day Sonny heard

the same sounds.
The auto plant
was a loud place.
The machine shop
was one of the loudest parts
of the plant.
Sonny kept plugs
in his ears
to shut out some noise
and save his hearing.

"Don't forget
the meeting today,"
called the guy
down the line.

"What time?"
asked Sonny.

"3:00 p.m.
You better be there.
I hear
it's pretty important."

"What's it about?"
Sonny asked.

"I don't know,"
shouted the guy.
"But we've got
to be there."

"I'll be there,"
said Sonny.

At 3:00
the buzz-click stopped.
The noise
on the shop floor
came to an end.
Sonny took off his cap,
wiped his head,
and put the cap back on.
"Another day,
another dollar!"
he laughed.

All the workers
walked off the floor.
They headed
toward the meeting room.
They laughed and talked
as they walked.
They could not have guessed
what they were about to hear.

Thinking It Over

1. What do you think
   are some reasons
   why Sonny hates his job?

2. What would you do
   if you didn't like
   your job?

3. What would you guess
   the workers will hear
   at the meeting?

CHAPTER 2

A small crowd
was gathering
in the meeting room.
All the workers
found a seat.
It was time
for the meeting
to start.

The person
who stood up to speak
was not Sonny's boss.
It was the man in charge
of the machine shop.
"This must be
really important,"
Sonny said to himself.

"As you know,
times change,"
said the man.
"Just think
how your grandparents lived.
They didn't have
the machines
that make your life better.
Well, new machines
can help out
in this plant, too.
I'm talking
about robots.
Now, robots are
good in some ways
and bad in others.
They are good
because they can do
some very hard jobs.
They are bad
because your jobs
will no longer be needed."

The whole room
let out a gasp.

Everyone
was shocked.

"You mean
we're laid off?"
asked one woman.

"I'm afraid so,"
said the man in charge.
"You see, your jobs
will never again
be filled by people.
Our new robots
can do your jobs
in much less time.
And robots don't
make mistakes.
They don't
take sick days, either.
Robots will be better
for these kinds of jobs."

"What about us people?"
shouted a woman
in the back.

"You workers
can file
for unemployment checks,"
said the man in charge.
"Maybe we can call
some of you back
for a different job.
Or maybe
some of you will find
even better jobs
with other companies."

Sonny could hardly speak.
He wished
he had never said
all those bad things
about his job.
This work
was a lot better
than no work at all.

How would he
tell his family?
How would they

make ends meet?
Where would he
find another job?
He was 45 years old.
Who would hire him?
He had worked
at the same job
for the last 18 years.

And think of it!
To have your job
taken over
by a robot!
Not even
a real person!
Sonny felt
all alone.
He felt
like a piece of dirt
on the street.
He felt like
nothing at all.

Thinking It Over

1. How would you feel
   if your job
   were taken over
   by a machine?

2. Is it ever fair
   to lay off workers?
   If yes,
   when is it fair?

3. If you got laid off,
   how would you
   cut down
   on spending?

CHAPTER **3**

"You go on
without me,"
Sonny told his friend
from the car pool.
"I'd rather walk."
He was angry
at the company.
He felt like hitting
someone or something.
He wanted
to be alone
for a little while
before he got home.

And he had
some thinking to do.
He had to decide
how to tell
his family.
He had to think of ways
they could cut down

on spending.
The unemployment checks
would never cover everything.

He knew
he could not wait
for the machine shop
to call him back.
That might never happen.
He must find a job—
and soon.
He also knew
it would not be easy.
He pictured himself
going from plant to plant.
He could just hear
them saying,
"Sorry,
we're not hiring."

He went
over and over
all these things
in his mind.
He felt terrible.

When he got home,
he was still angry.
But the thinking time
had helped him
sort things out.

He didn't say hello
to his wife, Lois.
He just sat down
at the kitchen table.
He put his head
in his hands.

"What's the matter?"
asked Lois.

"I'm finished,"
said Sonny softly.

"What do you mean,
you're finished?"
Lois wanted to know.

"I got laid off,"
said Sonny.

"I lost my job
to a robot.
Now, how's that
for a kick in the rear?"

At first,
Lois didn't know
what to say.
Then she spoke.
"You never liked
your job anyway,"
she said.

"I liked it better
than no job at all,"
Sonny said.

"You'll find
another job,"
Lois said.
She was trying
to make her husband
feel better.
She was trying

to make herself
feel better, too.

"Maybe,"
said Sonny.
"And maybe not.
But, right now,
we have to make
some big changes
around here.
We have to learn
to live on less."

"We will,"
said Lois.
"I know we can.
Pretty soon
you'll be working again.
And everything
will be fine."

Lois wasn't sure
she believed
her own words.

But she had to try.
She and Sonny
had three kids
to feed.
She had to believe
they could weather this storm.

Thinking It Over

1. Why does Sonny
   feel so bad?

2. Have you ever said something
   just to make someone
   feel better?

3. How well do you
   weather storms
   in your life?

CHAPTER 4

Sonny went
to the state job office.
He had to file
for unemployment checks.

He waited in line.
"What am I
doing here?"
he said to himself.
"What kind of man
gets laid off?
What kind of man
has to wait in line
for a handout?"

Then it was
his turn.
A man
asked Sonny
a lot of questions.

"How long did you
work in the machine shop?"
the man asked.
"Why were you
laid off?"
"May I see
your birth record?"
"Are you married?"
"Does your wife
hold a job?"
"How many children
do you have?"
"What kind of job
will you be looking for?"

Sonny answered everything.
Then he said,
"You know,
I don't like handouts.
I would rather work
for my money."

"It's not a handout,"
the man said.
"When you were working,

you were paying
into the unemployment fund.
Now you will get back
some of that money
because you got laid off.
It's only fair."

The man
gave Sonny
a few job leads.
Sonny left the office
with his head down.
"It may be money
I should have,"
he said to himself.
"But I'd still rather
work for it."

Thinking It Over

1. What is your idea
   about handouts?
   Are there times
   when you would take one?

2. Would you rather
   get an unemployment check
   or be working for your money?

3. Have you ever
   been laid off?
   How does it feel
   to wait in line
   for unemployment?

CHAPTER 5

The first unemployment check
did not come
for three weeks.
It was a long wait.
And the check
was not as big
as it was
when Sonny was working.

The next few weeks
were hard on Sonny
and the whole family.
Money was tight.
The three kids
were getting
under Sonny's skin.
He was feeling low.
He didn't have
enough to keep busy.

"Why don't you
fix the sink?"
Lois asked Sonny.

"Don't feel like it,"
he told her.

He sat around
and watched
a lot of TV.
He drank
too much beer.
It was hard for him
to crack a smile.
He didn't even want
to see his old friends
from the machine shop.

"You're going
to have to get out
and look for a job,"
Lois told him
one day.
"You must show up

at the job service.
You must show them
that you are trying
to find a new job."

"Get off my back!"
Sonny yelled.
"There is no job
out there for me.
Why go to the trouble
of looking?"

"You know what
your trouble is, Sonny?"
Lois asked.
"You are feeling sorry
for yourself.
So what
if a robot
took your job?
A robot
might be able
to drill bolt holes.
But no robot

could ever be
as good a person
as you are.
Don't you see?"

"I see,"
said Sonny.
"I see I'm no good.
I'm going away
for a few days.
I need to do
a little fishing.
Where's my tent?"

Thinking It Over

1. Have you ever had
   too much time
   on your hands?
   How did you
   pass the time?

2. Do you ever
   feel sorry for yourself?
   If so, why?

3. For what reasons
   would a person
   feel "no good"?

4. What do you do
   when you're feeling bad
   about yourself?

CHAPTER 6

Sonny stood
knee-deep
in the stream.
The afternoon sun
shone on the water.
He hadn't
caught a fish
since morning.
He hadn't even
felt a bite.

Just then,
there was a bite
on the line.
It felt
like a big fish
making a strong pull.
Sonny pulled up
on his rod

and hooked the fish.
Just at that second,
an idea came to him.
He seemed
to catch hold of himself
as well as the fish.
"That's it!"
he said out loud.
"I'm going to find
a new job.
I can't wait around
another day."

Sonny packed up
his fishing gear.
He folded up
the tent.
He drove
to the auto plant.
He didn't even stop
at home first.

He parked
in front of the

employment office.
He marched inside.

"I'm here
for a new job,"
he told the woman
at the desk.
"I got laid off
from the machine shop.
This is a big company.
You must
find a place for me
somewhere else.
I can't wait forever."

The woman
put down her pen.
"I'll see
what I can do,"
she said.
She made
a few phone calls.
Then she turned
to Sonny.

"Can you weld?"
she asked.

Sonny remembered
how he used to
hate welding.
But he said,
"Yes, I can weld."

"This is
your lucky day,"
the woman said
as she wrote down a name.
"A welder
in the assembly plant
quit this morning.
They need someone
right away.
A man named Curt Bobson
is the boss there.
You go over
to Building G.
He will be waiting
to talk to you."

Thinking It Over

1. When Sonny
   caught the fish,
   he seemed to also
   catch hold of himself.
   Has an "eye-opener" like this
   ever happened to you?

2. Would you have the heart
   to march in
   and tell someone
   to give you a job?
   Why or why not?

3. What are some good ways
   to find a job?

CHAPTER 7

The next Monday morning
Sonny went to work
in the assembly plant.
This is where
the cars
were put together.

Sonny's new job
was to weld together
the steel beams
that made up
each car's frame.
It was not
easy work.
Bits of fire
flew all around him.
He had to wear
a hot mask.
But Sonny

was very happy
just to be working again.
He had a new job,
a new boss,
and a new way
of looking at life.
He even fixed
that sink
at home.

Lois and the kids
were happy, too.
Lois went out
and bought the kids
the new winter coats
they needed.
She had been
putting that off
until Sonny found a job.

For the first time
in his life,
Sonny enjoyed welding.
He liked

watching the cars
come together.
As he finished
welding each frame,
it would move
down the line
on a long belt
above the workers.
The car engines
would come in
on another line.
The engines and frames
would come together
just past Sonny.
Workers down the line
would drop the engine
into the frame.
Together,
the two pieces
would move along
to the final assembly line.

As Sonny watched,
it crossed his mind

that robots
could be doing
some of these jobs
better than people could.
That idea
made him afraid.
Why, he wondered,
were people
still doing these hard jobs?

   He got his answer
two months later.

Thinking It Over

1. Would you be happy
   to be working,
   even if you didn't really like
   the job?

2. In any jobs
   you have had,
   what parts of the job
   were most interesting to you?

3. Has anything
   ever happened to you
   that gave you
   a new way
   of looking at life?

CHAPTER 8

Sonny waited
for the bad news.
He waited to hear,
"Your job
will be filled
by a robot.
You are laid off."

But that
was not quite
what he heard.

"Your job
will be filled
by a robot,"
Curt Bobson began.
"But you
are not laid off.
The company
wants to train you
for a new job."

"What new job?"
asked Sonny.

"We need people
to check and fix
the robots,"
said Curt.
"If a robot goes down,
we're in trouble.
We need to make sure
every robot
stays in tip-top shape
at all times.
We would like
to train you
to go around
checking robots.
If something is wrong,
you will fix it."

"You mean
you'll send me
to school?"
Sonny asked.

"Sort of, yes,"
said Curt.
"Your line boss
will learn all about robots
from the company
that makes them.
He will then
train you
and the others.
He will show you
everything you need to know
about the robots."

"How long
will it take?"
Sonny asked.

"This is
a very complete
training program,"
Curt said.
"You will train
for 1,000 hours.
At 40 hours a week,

that will take
about six months."

"Half a year?"
Sonny asked.
"That's a long time.
Will I be paid
during that time?"

"Of course,"
said Curt.
"So what do you think?
We believe
you can do it.
Would you like
to become
a robot service worker?"

"I don't know,"
said Sonny.
"I haven't been to school
for so many years.
Would you let me
think about it?"

"Sure,"
Curt said.
"But remember,
training for the new job
is the only way
we can keep you here.
Remember, too,
this job
will be cleaner
and much more interesting."

"Right,"
said Sonny.

He understood
what Curt was telling him.
But he didn't know
how he could train
for half a year.
He was afraid
the new work
would be too hard.
He could not see himself
learning a whole new job.

Thinking It Over

1. What do you think
   of a company
   that cuts out your job
   but wants to teach you
   a new job?

2. What would you think
   if you were given the chance
   to train for a new job?

3. What are
   the best and worst things
   about learning new skills?

CHAPTER 9

"So that's the story,"
Sonny told Lois.
"I learn a new job
or I'm out.
What will I do?
I can't go to school
all day,
every day,
for half a year!"

"Why not?"
asked Lois.
"What are you
afraid of?"

"Nothing,"
Sonny lied.
"I just don't want
to sit in school."

"I don't think
it's a matter
of sitting in school,"
said Lois.
"The way you tell it,
it will be
hands-on learning.
What's wrong
with that?"

"I'm no kid,"
Sonny said.
"We both know that.
For almost 30 years
I've been
a working man.
I'm the kind of guy
who gets down and dirty.
I need to work
with my hands.
I'm not one
to work with fancy ideas
in my head."

"The new job
would let you
work with your hands
and your head,"
Lois said.
"Besides,
where else
could you go now?
This is
what the company
is willing to give you."

"That's just it,"
said Sonny.
"I don't have
any choice.
I'm going
to have to do
this training thing.
Either that
or we don't eat.
I have to go.
And that's that."

Thinking It Over

1. Suppose you have a problem.
   How can talking it over
   with someone
   help you decide
   what to do?

2. Do you work best
   with your head
   or your hands?

3. How do you learn best—
   • by listening to someone
     talk?
   • by watching someone
     do something? or
   • by trying it out yourself?

CHAPTER 10

The training program
was nothing like school
as Sonny remembered it.
For one thing,
the trainer
was Sonny's line boss.
He had learned
about the new robots.
He was ready
to pass on
what he knew.

For another thing,
this was not
a large class.
The only students
were Sonny
and three other line workers.

The four of them
and the boss
would become a team.

The training book
was full of pictures.
It was easy to see
what the trainer
was trying to explain.

There were even videos
to watch and listen to.

But much of the time
was spent
on the floor.
The trainer
and the four workers
looked inside the robots.
They saw for themselves
how the robots worked.
They learned
how to spot trouble.
They tried

fixing little problems
before they became
big problems.

Sonny found the robots
very interesting.
Most interesting of all
was the robot
that took over
his welding job.
It didn't look
much like a person.
Its body
was shaped
like a drum.
A long metal arm
came up from the drum.
There were
wires and tubes
growing out of the arm
like vines.
The arm bent
in three places.
At the end of the arm

were two metal fingers.
Sonny watched the fingers
hold the welding gun
just as a person would.

The welding robot
worked fast.
It could get
into places
that Sonny
always had trouble reaching.
It didn't mind
the heat
or the bits
of flying fire.
And it did its job
right every time.

Best of all,
Sonny learned
to understand
how the robot worked.
Day by day,
he came to know the robot

better and better.
He sometimes felt
as if the robot
were his friend.

Sonny also enjoyed
working with the team.
The line boss
worked the computer
that ran the robots.
The other four
took care
of the robots
that welded car frames.
If a robot
was having a problem,
everyone on the team
would talk it over.
If one person
didn't know the answer,
someone else did.
Within a few months,
they knew
just what to do.

Thinking It Over

1. In what ways
   are people
   better than machines?

2. In what ways
   are machines
   better than people?

3. Is it better
   to fix something
   when it breaks
   or to keep it from breaking
   in the first place?

CHAPTER 11

The training time
went fast.
After six months,
Sonny's team
of robot service workers
was working
up to speed.

"You did it, Sonny,"
said Lois
on the last day
of training.
"You said
you couldn't,
but you did."

"Yes, I did,"
said Sonny.
He was feeling
pretty good
about himself

these days.
"Not a bad trick
for an old dog,"
he laughed.

"You're not old,"
said Lois.

"I'm old enough,"
he said.

Lois put her arms
around her husband.
"Old enough for what?"
she asked.

"Old enough
to know better,"
said Sonny.

"I still don't know
what you're talking about,"
Lois said.

"I should have known
that getting laid off
is not the end
of the world,"
Sonny said.
"I should have known
that there is always
something new
to learn.
I should have known
that I wasn't too old
to learn something new.
Now it's time
for me
to go to work,
my dear."

Lois gave Sonny
a little kiss.
"You really enjoyed
the training,
didn't you?"
she asked.

"You know what?"
Sonny answered.
"I really did."

"Are you sorry
this is the end?"
Lois asked him.

"The end?"
he laughed.
"This isn't the end.
This is just the beginning.
This is the start
of a whole new job.
This is the start
of a whole new time
in my life.
The only thing
this is the end of
is me
on the assembly line.
I just joined
the work force
of tomorrow!"

"Get out of here,
big shot!"
smiled Lois.
"Go take a walk
into the future!"

"I'll do that,"
said Sonny.
"See you
when I get home."

He walked
out the door.
Then he looked back
and gave Lois
a big "thumbs up."

Thinking It Over

1. What makes you
    feel really good
    about yourself?
    How do you show it?

2. Do you believe,
    in a manner of speaking,
    that an old dog
    can be taught
    new tricks?

3. How can you be ready
    to join "the work force
    of tomorrow"?